DEDICATION

For my three boys, whose
love of golf inspired this story.

www.mascotbooks.com

The Little Aces, A Golf Story

©2017 Rose Ostrow. All Rights Reserved. No part of this publication may be reproduced, stored in a retrieval system or transmitted in any form by any means electronic, mechanical, or photocopying, recording or otherwise without the permission of the author.

Fourth printing. This Mascot Books edition printed in 2020.

For more information, please contact:
Mascot Books
620 Herndon Parkway #320
Herndon, VA 20170
info@mascotbooks.com

Library of Congress Control Number: 2017902089

CPSIA Code: PRT0317D
ISBN-13: 978-1-68401-051-6

Printed in the United States

The Little Aces
A Golf Story

Written by Rose Ostrow

Illustrated by Nazar Horokhivskyi

Julian and Eli were brothers who loved to play golf together.
Whether warm or chilly, they played no matter the weather.
On weekends they joined their dad on the golf course,
Where they practiced hitting drives with great force.

To get the ball in the hole eighteen times is the goal of the game,
And to do it with the fewest strokes requires great aim.
Once the boys finished hitting drives, they headed to the green
To practice their putting before playing eighteen.

During one of their games, Eli hit the ball FAR and away.
Both boys watched it go right down the fairway.

Julian hit next and watched his ball fly straight.
Eli said, "Wow Julian, that shot was great!"
The boys put their clubs away and jumped into the golf cart.
Seemed like they were both off to a pretty good start.

Driving up the fairway they found Eli's ball,
But they didn't see Julian's and exclaimed, "Where did it fall?"
"It looked like it went straight, so it should be right here.
We'll find it, Julian," said Eli. "Please, have no fear!"

The boys SEARCHED and SEARCHED but nothing was found.
"The ball is gone! Game over!" they both frowned.

Suddenly, a chipmunk ran by with something round in his cheek.
"Catch him, quickly!" Julian said. "He's on his way to the creek!"
"Chipmunk, chipmunk," Eli cried, "won't you give us our ball back?
We need it to get our game on track."

"THIS ISN'T YOUR BALL, boys, it's a bunch of acorns I'm eating. Now let me go on my way! I'm late to a meeting."

Next, the boys saw a rabbit hop by in a hurry.
He was gray and white and extremely furry.
"Rabbit, rabbit," they cried, "won't you give us our ball back?
We need it to get our game on track."

"Why, THIS ISN'T YOUR BALL, it's my white bushy tail. But keep searching for it! I'm sure you won't fail."

"There's our ball!" shouted Julian. "In the nest atop that tree!"
"We found it, we found it," the boys shouted with glee.
"Birdy, birdy," they cried, "won't you give us our ball back?
We need it to get our game on track."

"Why, THIS ISN'T YOUR BALL. It's my egg that's about to hatch!
I hope you find it though, so you can get on with your match."

Next, the boys saw a snake with a lump in his midsection.
They kept a fair distance, for their own protection.
"Snake, snake, won't you give us our ball back?
We need it to get our game on track."

"Sssssssssssss...THIS ISN'T YOUR BALL, it's a mouse I just ate.
And if you don't watch out, you'll share the same fate."

"Look over there! I think I see my ball by that tree."
The boys ran over quickly to see.
What they found was indeed hard and round,
And laying near the green on the ground.

"I'M NOT YOUR BALL, boys, that's my shell you saw.
I'm Mr. Thomas, a turtle," he said while extending his claw.

"Could it be that my ball is still up in the air?"
Julian asked, pointing to the sky with despair.
Eli looked up and saw a great big bald eagle
Flying high over the course and looking very regal.

"Eagle, eagle, won't you please give us our ball back?
We need it to get our game on track."

The eagle flew down quickly. "THIS ISN'T YOUR BALL, you see.
That's my bald white head, boys. Now please let me be."

Julian turned to Eli and said, "Please just continue to play. My ball will turn up. Don't let it ruin your day.

I can lose a stroke and play with a new golf ball. I think those are the rules, if I recall."

Eli agreed and CHIPPED his ball onto the green.
He grabbed his putter to finish the first hole of eighteen.

The ball went in and they heard a loud TOCK!
When they looked in the hole, they got a real shock!

That sound was Eli's ball hitting Julian's in the hole.
Julian quickly removed both balls, along with the flag pole.
"That's my ball! I must have gotten a hole in one!
And here we thought my ball was gone!"

Julian and Eli's dad was concerned with the boys gone so long.
He drove around the course, expecting them to be further along.
He kept backtracking until he found them on the first hole's green
And said, "Boys, I've been worried! Where have you been?"

The boys shouted at the same time. "JULIAN GOT AN ACE!"
A shocked look appeared on their dad's face.
They began to explain how the ball went missing
And how they met a bunny, a turtle, and a snake that was hissing.
Their dad said, "No way! What an amazing feat!

Getting a hole in one really can't be beat!"

Dad lifted both boys up and spun them around
And said, "I love your story of the lost ball that was found."
Eli and Julian jumped from his arms and gave each other a high five.
Then they ran off to the next hole, hoping for another amazing drive.

About the Author

Rose Ostrow was introduced to the game of golf by her husband when they first met. However, it was after her two boys began to play that Rose's interest in the sport grew. Spending hours on the golf course with her husband and sons inspired her to write her first book, *The Little Aces, A Golf Story.*

Rose lives in New York City with her husband and two sons.